What Dinah Saw

Written by Maureen Haselhurst

Illustrated by Korky Paul

D1303754

Winnona Park
Elementary School

Dinah saw a dinosaur
in a cave down by the sea.
He waved his giant dino paw
and asked her in for tea.

You can't ignore a dinosaur
with a spike upon his nose,
and claws as sharp as dino saws
that peep out from his toes!

He sadly shambled down the shore
and sat down on the rocks,
and Dinah saw the dino wore
a pair of striped socks.

"I'm just a lonely dino bore,
so come and play," he begged.
"No one comes here anymore.
There's just me and my egg!"

3

She put her hand into his paw,
"Of course I'll come to tea.
Now, piggyback me to your door.
Your playmate can be me!"

They piggybacked along the shore.
They danced among the waves.
Then the dino took her to his door
and she peeped into his cave.

A roof of pearl, a green glass floor,
and walls of sea-blue stones—
all glittered like a treasure store.
This was the dino's home!

Dinah went off to explore
and found a giant crib,
with the biggest egg you ever saw,
dressed in a bonnet and bib.

The dino stroked it with his paw
and proudly rocked the cot.
Dinah whispered, "Is it yours?"
He said, "It's all I've got."

"There once were dinosaurs galore,
but everything went wrong.
There was snow and ice and winds that roared,
and all my friends were gone!"

"It froze their horns, it froze their paws,
and their toes were icy blocks.
But *I* was snug because I wore
my cozy striped socks!"

"I kept my egg inside my jaws,
where it was snug and warm,
and waited for the ice to thaw
and my baby to be born."

"I spent a million years or more
knitting baby socks and mitts.
But knitting is an awful chore,
I hope that each pair fits."

"I made my babe a seesaw
and I made a merry-go-round.
Such fun toys just waiting for
my babe to make a sound."

"But I still can't hatch my dinosaur.
I've hugged my egg so tight.
I've tried until I'm dino sore—
that egg needs dynamite!"

"Hatching eggs is such a bore!
It's very, very slow.
I just can't do it anymore!
Will *you* have a go?"

Dinah said, "Poor dinosaur,
of course I'll have a try.
I haven't hatched an egg before.
Shall I sing a lullaby?"

The dino's head flopped in his paws.
He rocked back in his chair.
He fell asleep and dino snores
thundered through the air.

They echoed on the glassy floor.
They boomed along the walls.
They rattled off the dino's door,
but the egg ignored it all.

11

Dinah sang until her throat was sore.
She told it funny jokes.
She tap-danced on the glassy floor
and the dinosaur awoke.

Dinah said, "I'm getting bored.
Come on, egg. Please hatch out.
You've got a dad you'll just adore,
come on—don't hang about!"

Then, suddenly a crack—a claw!
The sound of gurgling cries.
The baby gave a tiny roar,
"Hi, Dad! Surprise, surprise!"

The dino gave a happy roar,
"Hello, my little lad.
Come on! What are you waiting for?
Come on and hug your dad!"

They seesawed on the seashore.
They played among the rocks,
and on his paws the baby wore
a pair of striped socks.

The baby held his daddy's paw,
and toddled to the sea.
"There's a big, wide world we must explore,
my little one and me."

Dinah saw the dinos soar
beyond the setting sun,
to seek some other dinosaurs
and perhaps a dino mom.